HORRID HENRY
and the
Abominable Snowman

HORRID HENRY
and the
Abominable
Snowman

Francesca Simon
Illustrated by Tony Ross

Orion
Children's Books

Horrid Henry and the Abominable Snowman
first published in Great Britain in 2007
by Orion Children's Books
This edition published in Great Britain in 2015
by Orion Children's Books
an imprint of Hachette Children's Group
a division of Hodder and Stoughton Ltd
Carmelite House
5o Victoria Embankment
London EC4Y 0DZ
An Hachette UK company

1 3 5 7 9 10 8 6 4 2

Text © Francesca Simon 2007
Illustrations © Tony Ross 2015

The right of Francesca Simon and Tony Ross to be identified
as author and illustrator of this work has been asserted.

ISBN 978 1 4440 0909 5

A catalogue record for this book is available from the British Library.

Printed in China

www.orionchildrensbooks.com
www.horridhenry.co.uk

There are many more
Horrid Henry Early Reader books available.

For a complete list visit:
www.orionchildrensbooks.com
or
www.horridhenry.co.uk

Contents

Chapter 1

Moody Margaret took aim.
Thwack!

A snowball whizzed past and smacked
Sour Susan in the face.
"AAAAARRGGHHH!"
shrieked Susan.

"Ha ha, got you," said Margaret.

"You big meanie," howled Susan,
scooping up a fistful of snow and
hurling it at Margaret.

Thwack!

Susan's snowball smacked
Moody Margaret in the face.
"OWWWW!" screamed Margaret.
"You've blinded me!"

"Good!" screamed Susan.

"I hate you!"
shouted Margaret, shoving Susan.

"I hate you more!"
shouted Susan, pushing Margaret.

Splat!

Margaret toppled into the snow.

Splat!

Susan toppled into the snow.

"I'm going home to build
my own snowman," sobbed Susan.

"Fine. I'll win
without you,"
said Margaret.

"Won't!"

"Will! I'm going to win, copycat," shrieked Margaret.

"I'm going to win," shrieked Susan. "I kept my best ideas secret."

Chapter 2

"Win? Win what?"
demanded Horrid Henry,
stomping down his front steps
in his snow boots and swaggering
over. Henry could hear the word
win from miles away.

"Haven't you heard about the competition?" said Sour Susan. "The prize is—"

"Shut up! Don't tell him," shouted Moody Margaret, packing snow onto her snowman's head.

Win?
Competition?
Prize?

Horrid Henry's ears quivered. What secret were they trying to keep from him? Well, not for long. Horrid Henry was an expert at extracting information.

"Oh, the competition. I know all about that," lied Horrid Henry.

"Hey, great snowman,"
he added, strolling casually over to
Margaret's snowman and pretending
to admire her work.
Now, what should he do?
Torture?

Margaret's ponytail was always
a tempting target.

And snow
down her
jumper would
make her talk.

What about blackmail?
He could spread some rumours
about Margaret at school. Or . . .

"Tell me about the competition
or the ice guy gets it,"
said Horrid Henry suddenly, leaping
over to the snowman and putting his
hands around its neck.

"You wouldn't dare,"
gasped Moody Margaret.
Henry's mittened hands
got ready to push.

"Bye bye, head," hissed Horrid Henry.
"Nice knowing you."

Margaret's snowman wobbled.
"Stop!" screamed Margaret.
I'll tell you. It doesn't matter
'cause you'll never win."

"Keep talking," said Horrid Henry
warily, watching out in case Susan
tried to ambush him from behind.

"Frosty Freeze are having
a best snowman competition,"
said Moody Margaret, glaring.
"The winner gets a year's free supply
of ice cream. The judges will decide
tomorrow morning. Now get away
from my snowman."

Chapter 3

Horrid Henry walked off in a daze,
his jaw dropping.
Margaret and Susan pelted him
with snowballs but Henry didn't
even notice.

Free ice cream for a year direct from
the Frosty Freeze Ice Cream factory.

Oh wow!

Horrid Henry couldn't believe it.
Mum and Dad were so mean and
horrible they hardly ever let him
have ice cream.

And when they did, they never
ever let him put on his own
hot chocolate fudge sauce and
whipped cream and sprinkles.
Or even scoop the ice cream himself.
Oh no.

Well, when he won the Best
Snowman Competition
they couldn't stop him gorging
on Chunky Chocolate Fab Fudge
Caramel Delight, or Vanilla Whip
Tutti-Fruitti Toffee Treat. Oh boy!

Henry could taste that glorious ice cream now.

He'd live on ice cream.

He'd bathe in ice cream.

He'd sleep in ice cream.

Everyone from school would
turn up at his house when the
Frosty Freeze truck arrived bringing
his weekly barrels. No matter how
much they begged, Horrid Henry
would send them all away.
No way was he sharing a drop of
his precious ice cream with anyone.

And all he had to do was to build
the best snowman in the
neighbourhood. Pah!
Henry's was sure to be the winner.
He would build the biggest
snowman of all.
And not just a snowman.

A snowman with claws,
and horns, and fangs.
A vampire-demon-monster snowman.
An Abominable Snowman.

Yes!

Henry watched Margaret and
Susan rolling the snow and packing
their saggy snowman.
Ha. Snow heap, more like.

"You'll never win with that,"
jeered Horrid Henry.
"Your snowman is pathetic."

"Better than yours,"
snapped Margaret.

Horrid Henry rolled his eyes.
"Obviously, because I haven't started
mine yet."

"We've got a big head start on you,
so ha ha ha," said Susan.
"We're building a ballerina snowgirl."

"Shut up, Susan,"
screamed Margaret.

A ballerina snowgirl?
What a stupid idea. If that was
the best they could do
Henry was sure to win.

"Mine will be the biggest, the best,
the most gigantic snowman ever
seen," said Horrid Henry. "And much
better than your stupid snow dwarf."

"Fat chance," sneered Margaret.

"Yeah, Henry," sneered Susan.
"Ours is the best."

"No way," said Horrid Henry,
starting to roll a gigantic ball
of snow for Abominable's big belly.

There was no time to lose.

Chapter 4

Roll. Roll. Roll.

Up the path, down the path,
across the garden, down the side,
back and forth, back and forth,
Horrid Henry rolled the
biggest ball of snow ever seen.

"Henry, can I build a snowman
with you?" came a little voice.

"No," said Henry, starting to carve
out some clawed feet.

"Oh please," said Peter.
"We could build a great big one
together. Like a bunny snowman,
or a—"

"No!" said Henry.
"It's my snowman. Build your own."

"Muuuuummmm!" wailed Peter.
"Henry won't let me build a
snowman with him."

"Don't be horrid, Henry," said Mum.
"Why don't you build one together?"

"NO!!!" said Horrid Henry.
He wanted to make his own snowman.
If he built a snowman with
his stupid worm brother,
he'd have to share the prize.

Well, no way.
He wanted all that ice cream
for himself. And his Abominable
Snowman was sure to be the best.
Why share a prize when you
didn't have to?

"Get away from my snowman, Peter,"
hissed Henry.

Perfect Peter snivelled. Then he
started to roll a tiny ball of snow.

"And get your own snow," said Henry.
"All this is mine."

"Muuuuum!" wailed Peter.
"Henry's hogging all the snow."

Chapter 5

"We're done," trilled Moody Margaret. "Beat this if you can." Horrid Henry looked at Margaret and Susan's snowgirl, complete with a big pink tutu wound round the waist. It was as big as Margaret.

"That old heap of snow is nothing
compared to mine,"
bragged Horrid Henry.
Moody Margaret and Sour Susan
looked at Henry's Abominable
Snowman, complete with
Viking horned helmet, fangs,
and hairy scary claws. It was a few
centimetres taller than Henry.

"Nah nah ne nah nah, mine's bigger,"

boasted Henry.

"Nah nah ne nah nah, mine's better,"

boasted Margaret.

"How do you like my snowman?"
said Peter.
"Do you think I could win?"

Horrid Henry stared at
Perfect Peter's tiny snowman.
It didn't even have a head, just a long,
thin, lump body with two stones
stuck in the top for eyes.

Horrid Henry howled
with laughter.

"That's the worst snowman
I've ever seen," said Henry.
"It doesn't even have a head.
That's a snow carrot."

"It's not," wailed Peter.
"It's a big bunny."

"Henry! Peter! Suppertime,"
called Mum.

Henry stuck
out his tongue
at Margaret.
"And don't you
dare touch my
snowman."

Margaret stuck
out her tongue
at Henry.
"And don't you
dare touch my
snowgirl."

"I'll be watching you, Margaret."

"I'll be watching you, Henry."

They glared at each other.

Chapter 6

Henry woke.
What was that noise?

Was Margaret sabotaging
his snowman?
Was Susan stealing his snow?
Horrid Henry dashed to the window.

Phew.
There was his Abominable Snowman,
big as ever, dwarfing every other
snowman in the street. Henry's was
definitely the biggest, and the best.

Umm boy, he could taste that
Triple Fudge Gooey Chocolate Chip
Peanut Butter Marshmallow Custard
ice cream right now.

Horrid Henry climbed back into bed.
A tiny doubt nagged him.
Was his snowman definitely bigger
than Margaret's?

'Course it was, thought Henry.
"Are you sure?" rumbled his tummy.
"Yeah," said Henry.
"Because I really want that ice
cream," growled his tummy.
"Why don't you double-check?"

Henry got out of bed.
He was sure his was bigger
and better than Margaret's.
He was absolutely sure his
was bigger and better.
But what if . . .
I can't sleep without checking,
thought Henry.

Tip toe.
Tip toe.
Tip toe.

Horrid Henry slipped out
of the front door.

The whole street was silent and
white and frosty. Every house had
a snowman in front. All of them
much smaller than Henry's,
he noted with satisfaction.

And there was his Abominable
Snowman looming up, Viking horns
scraping the sky. Horrid Henry
gazed proudly. Next to him was
Peter's pathetic pimple, with its
stupid black stones.
A snow lump, thought Henry.

Then he looked over at Margaret's
snowgirl. Maybe it had fallen down,
thought Henry hopefully.
And if it hadn't maybe he could
help it on its way. He looked again.
And again.

That evil fiend!
Margaret had sneaked an extra ball
of snow on top, complete with
a huge flowery hat.

That little cheater, thought
Horrid Henry indignantly.
She'd sneaked out after bedtime
and made hers bigger than his.
How dare she?
Well, he'd fix Margaret.
He'd add more snow to his right away.
Horrid Henry looked around.

Where could he find more snow?
He'd already used up every drop on
his front lawn to build his giant, and
no new snow had fallen.

Henry shivered. Brr, it was freezing. He needed more snow, and he needed it fast. His slippers were starting to feel very wet and cold.

Horrid Henry eyed
Peter's pathetic lump of snow.
Hmmn, thought Horrid Henry.
Hmmn, thought Horrid Henry again.
Well, it's not doing any good sitting
there, thought Henry.

Someone could trip over it.
Someone could hurt themselves.
In fact, Peter's snowlump was a
danger. He had to act fast before
someone fell over it and broke a leg.

Quickly, he scooped up Peter's
snowman and stacked it carefully
on top of his. Then standing on
his tippy toes, he balanced the
Abominable Snowman's
Viking horns on top.

Da dum!
Much better.
And much bigger than Margaret's.
Teeth chattering, Horrid Henry
sneaked back into his house and crept
into bed. Ice cream, here I come,
thought Horrid Henry.

Chapter 7

Ding dong.
Horrid Henry jumped out of bed.
What a morning to oversleep.

Perfect Peter ran and
opened the door.
"We're from the Frosty Freeze
Ice Cream Factory," said the man,
beaming. "And you've got the
winning snowman out front."

"I won!" screeched Horrid Henry.
"I won!" He tore down the stairs
and out the door.

Oh what a lovely lovely day.
The sky was blue.
The sun was shining . . . huh??

Horrid Henry looked around.
Horrid Henry's Abominable
Snowman was gone.
"Margaret!" screamed Henry.
"I'll kill you!"

But Moody Margaret's snowgirl
was gone too.

The Abominable Snowman's helmet
lay on its side on the ground.
All that was left of Henry's
snowman was … Peter's pimple,
with its two black stone eyes.
A big blue ribbon was pinned
to the top.

"But that's my snowman,"
said Perfect Peter.

But … but …" said Horrid Henry.

"You mean, I won?" said Peter.

"That's wonderful, Peter," said Mum.

"That's fantastic, Peter," said Dad.

"All the others melted,"
said the Frosty Freeze man.
"Yours was the only one left.
It must have been a giant."

"It was," howled Horrid Henry.

What are you going to read next?

Have more adventures with Horrid Henry,

or save the day with Anthony Ant!

Become a superhero with Monstar,

float off to sea with Algy,

or have your very own Pirates' Picnic.

Grow carrots with

Lottie and Dottie,

make magic with The Witch Dog,

and cast a spell with

The Three Little Magicians.

Enjoy all the Early Readers.